Horus the Peregrine Falcon
Catch the Pigeon

Text © John Miles
Illustrations © Barry Robson

Langford Press, 10 New Road,
Langtoft, Peterborough, PE6 9LE
www.langford-press.co.uk

A CIP Record for this book is
available from the British Library
ISBN 978-1-904078-66-1

Designed by MRM Graphics Ltd
Printed in Spain under the supervision
of MRM Graphics Ltd, Winslow

FALCON
TOWER CRANE SERVICES LTD

Horus the Peregrine Falcon sponsored by
Falcon Tower Crane Services Ltd

Horus the Peregrine Falcon

by John Miles
and
artwork by Barry Robson

Myweebooks

Langford Press

Horus the Peregrine Falcon

Mrs Peregrine could feel the movement in her eggs and hear the soft cheeps of her chicks hatching under her body. Soon, after two days apart, all four eggs will have hatched, leaving her with four white downy chicks. You would have thought they ought to have been born in 'Downing Street' not on the *Houses of Parliament* high up on *Victoria Tower!* When Dad flies in with a plucked pigeon he marvels at these newborn children. Mum soon takes control, taking the bird from him as she is so much bigger than he is, and starts to tear off very small pieces of meat for the chicks to swallow.

The view from the nest was amazing, looking across the River Thames onto a great wheel called *The London Eye.* You could also see *Lambeth Palace* and big red buses crossing *Westminster Bridge.* Horus would have to learn all the sites around London once he began to fly. First of all, though, it was a matter of survival in the nest with two sisters and a brother to compete with. The girls had an advantage, as they were bigger from the very beginning.

Feral pigeon, or the town pigeon if you like, is the main item on the menu for the peregrines as London is full of them. These pigeons are descendants of a bird called a rock dove, which people bred for food thousands of years ago. Later, the birds were reared for racing and not food so London's birds are a mixture of escaped racing birds and feral birds.

Large numbers of pigeons can cause quite serious problems by leaving

their droppings on buildings, especially where they are nesting or roosting. Each bird will produce about 12 kilograms of droppings every year. Altogether, this means The Boroughs of London get over one million kilos of poo a year! Pigeon droppings can also contain several diseases which can affect humans, with one called 'Pigeon Fanciers' Lung'. In addition to this, the acids present in their poo can damage stonework. This means that peregrines are doing London a big favour by removing some of the pigeons.

This plentiful supply of food means that Horus and his brother and sisters grow very fast until feathers start to grow and replace the down. These feathers start off as hard shiny quills but soon burst out into feathers which Horus has to preen with his bill to keep clean and

8

in shape if he is to fly from the nest. These young birds start life with brownish grey feathers compared to the blue-grey of their parents. Their flight feathers are also slightly longer so they can compete in the big world against adult birds.

Horus did not know how privileged he was to have such a name in his falcon family. The name was first known from a falcon god way back 5,000 years ago in Ancient Egypt. The people of Egypt were inspired by the speed of the falcon, which can reach 200 miles an hour. They worshipped this bird, which we think was a peregrine like Horus, and even built temples and created statues of their god. One statue showed Horus protecting the greatest king of Egypt: Ramses II. The Greeks and Romans who conquered Egypt around 2,500 years later continued this worship. One city was even called the 'city of the falcons'. Maybe the present-day London should be called that and the people should worship these falcons for the job they do with the pigeons!

Once the feathers are fully grown, the nest becomes a crowded place as the peregrine chicks want to practise flapping their wings ready for the big day when they fly away from the nest.

Horus is always being pushed around by his sisters. Being smaller, the males develop more quickly so they can leave the nest as soon as possible.

Flapping stops when Horus and his brother and sisters are scared by enormous birds passing overhead. "What a noise they make!" Horus exclaims. "What is that pale smoke coming out from behind?" he asked. All four tuck themselves into the nest while Mum just stands there wondering what all the fuss is about. They were seeing the planes flying to and from London's airports!

The great day came for Horus. It was a sunny morning with little wind. He was at the front of the nest flapping away when one of his sisters came up behind him and pushed him out into the blue yonder. Off he went, flapping like mad across the sky, to another part of the building, *Big Ben*. He landed on the little hand of the clock and thought he felt it move. The big hand was nearing twelve and suddenly there was an almighty bang as the clock struck the hour. Horus was off again, flying back towards the nest, landing on top of his sister who was pushed down in the nest. "Serves you right for pushing me out," Horus said.

17

It was not long before he
flew across the river,
landing on *The London Eye*.
People in a glass case were
looking up at him. Horus
stopped briefly, just long
enough to preen his
valuable feathers, to make
sure he could fly.

20

Dad came across the river carrying a pigeon. He screamed to Mum to come and get it from him. They performed a wonderful food pass, with Mum catching the pigeon in mid-air after Dad had dropped it for her. Horus knew this was food time and left *The Eye* and flew back to the nest. Two herring gulls chased him across the river. He was pushed closer to the water, but Dad came to the rescue, diving onto the gulls who squawked with anger.

2013

A few days later, it was not long before his brother and sisters joined him on the wing and the sky often had six peregrines flying over *The Houses of Parliament*. Peregrines have used London buildings such as *Westminster Abbey* and *St Paul's Cathedral* for a very long time. The world famous American naturalist, John James Audubon, said he saw peregrines on these two buildings when he came to London between 1826 and 1829.

The MPs and Lords housed in *The Houses of Parliament* have influenced the life of peregrines for a long time too. Some of these folk shoot red grouse on the moors in northern Britain. Because people are greedy and want to shoot lots of red grouse, hundreds of peregrines and other birds

of prey are killed each year because they might eat some red grouse first. Killing the peregrine and other birds of prey is against the law! Horus and his family will be safer staying around London!

Horus was starting to explore London and his first port of call was *Trafalgar Square*. It is named after a famous British battle in 1805 against a French and Spanish fleet of ships; Lord Nelson was the dying hero. His statue here in the *Square* makes an excellent perch for peregrines, especially as Horus can look down on many pigeons. Is this the day he will catch his first bird?

The *Square* was full of people with cameras clicking, and groups of tourists flocking more than the pigeons. "No, I will try somewhere else," Horus thought.

B ROBSON 13

He flew over *St James's Park*. He saw some funny birds called pelicans, and green parrots called ring-necked parakeets that seemed too fast for him to catch. A very large building with corgi dogs walking around a

huge garden was next. Horus had found *Buckingham Palace*. Here were some white doves called fantails. These looked easy meat. He dived into them and came out with a foot full of feathers. Catching birds is not that easy!

Next, it was downriver over *London Bridge* and onto the *Tower of London*.
Some large black birds were on the grass here. Surely, they were too big
for Horus to catch. He dived down on them but the poor birds could not
fly and the ravens just 'honked' at Horus as he passed over them.
Their wings had been clipped to prevent them leaving the tower. It is to
do with a superstition about the 'Royal Crown' of England falling if ravens
are missing from the Tower.

Horus soon passed the Shard and over *Canary Wharf* and the O2 Arena but food was what he wanted most of all, not just a sight-seeing trip. So he decided to fly back to the nest to see if Mum or Dad had brought anything back lately. He passed *Cleopatra's Needle*, which is an obelisk brought all the way from Egypt and put up on *Victoria Embankment*. Carved on it are images of birds of Egypt, in pictures that form letters (called hieroglyphs) in their ancient alphabet. There are several images of Horus there, as you will remember he was a god!

Derek Ratcliffe was the most significant British nature conservationist of the 20th Century. He was the one who realised that bad chemicals used in farming were destroying the egg shells of the peregrine and other birds. He told us all about this in his world famous book, 'The Peregrine Falcon'.

Places to see peregrines around London:
WWT London Wetland Centre, Battersea Power Station, Tate Modern – RSPB view-point. http://www.londonperegrines.com/

Present books in the series – *Kitty the Toon and Screamer the Swift*
Forthcoming books – *Gowk the Cuckoo, Mavis the Song Thrush, Tony the Tawny Owl, Odessa the Osprey, Glead the Red Kite* and many more.

Our sponsors – Falcon Cranes actually worked on the erection of a peregrine nesting box on Battersea power station. With their cranes they hauled the nest box up into position for the birds to use and it has been used every year since. http://falcon-crane-sales-hire-uk.com/